by
Dan & Jason

Simon & Schuster

First published in Great Britain in 2022 by Simon & Schuster UK Ltd

First published in the USA in 2021 by Simon & Schuster Books for Young Readers,
an imprint of Simon & Schuster Children's Publishing Division,
1230 Avenue of the Americas, New York, New York 10020

1 3 5 7 9 10 8 6 4 2

Simon & Schuster UK Ltd
1st Floor, 222 Gray's Inn Road
London
WC1X 8HB

www.simonandschuster.co.uk
www.simonandschuster.com.au
www.simonandschuster.co.in

Simon & Schuster Australia, Sydney
Simon & Schuster India, New Delhi

A CIP catalogue record for this book is available from the British Library.

PB ISBN 978-1-3985-1270-2
eBook ISBN 978-1-3985-1271-9

MIX
Paper from
responsible sources
FSC® C020056

For Harrison, Vivian,
Eloise, and Winona:
the most amazing Zerks
we've ever known.

P.S. Don't let the
"bed slugs" bite!

—D. & J.

24

THE WINDOW! IT'S YOUR ONLY CHANCE!

The one twenty feet off the ground!?

YOU GOT THIS!

Does she, though? It's so high up, and she's so small.

Heh, heh, heh, heh, heh.

And she'll have to get through me!

25

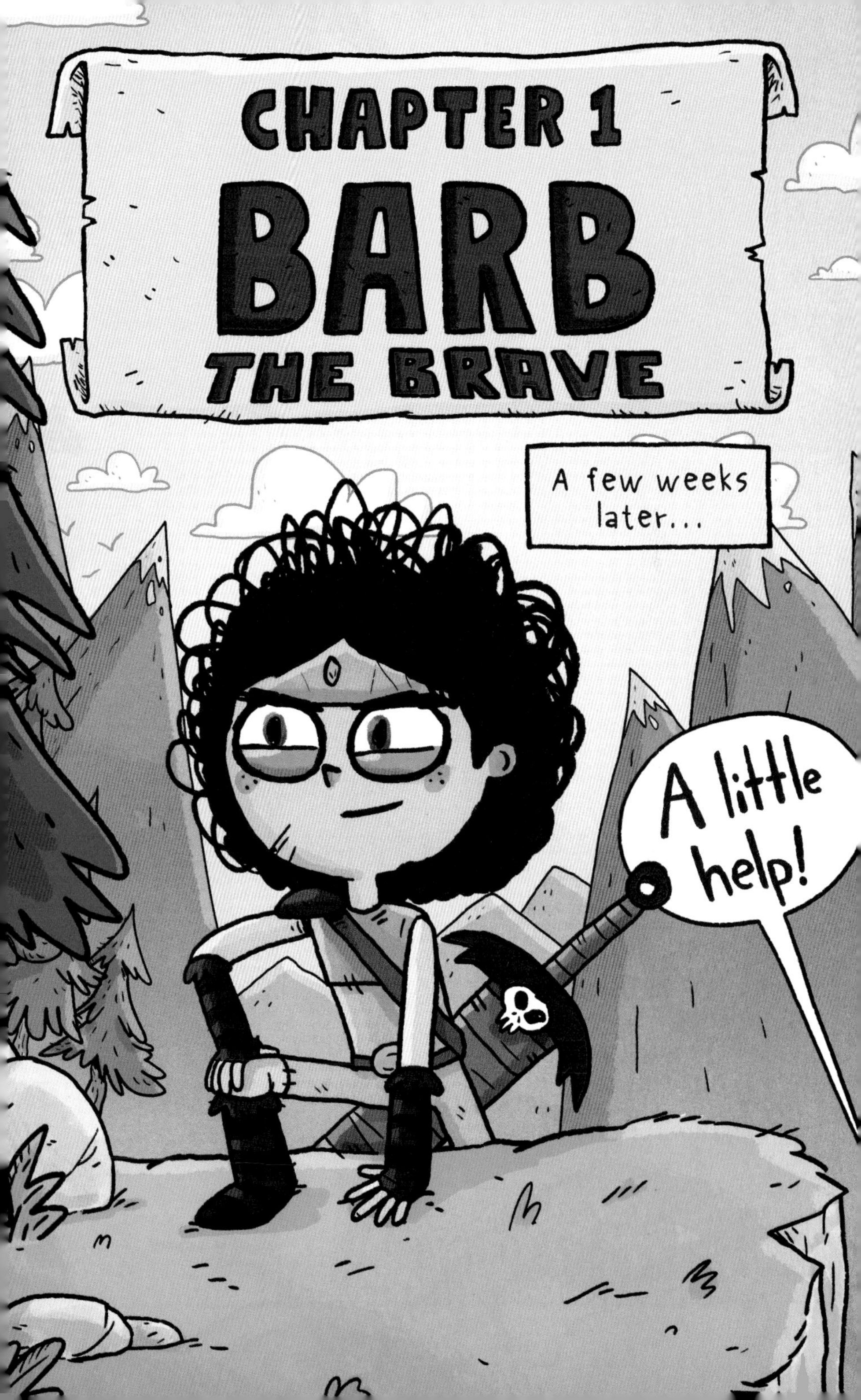
CHAPTER 1
BARB THE BRAVE
A few weeks later...
A little help!

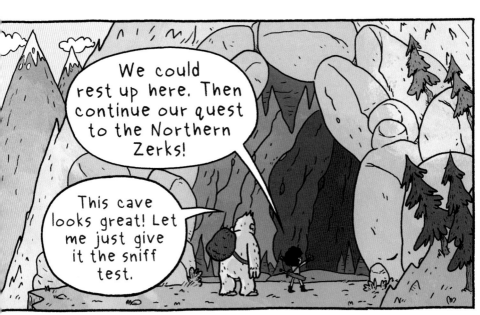

34

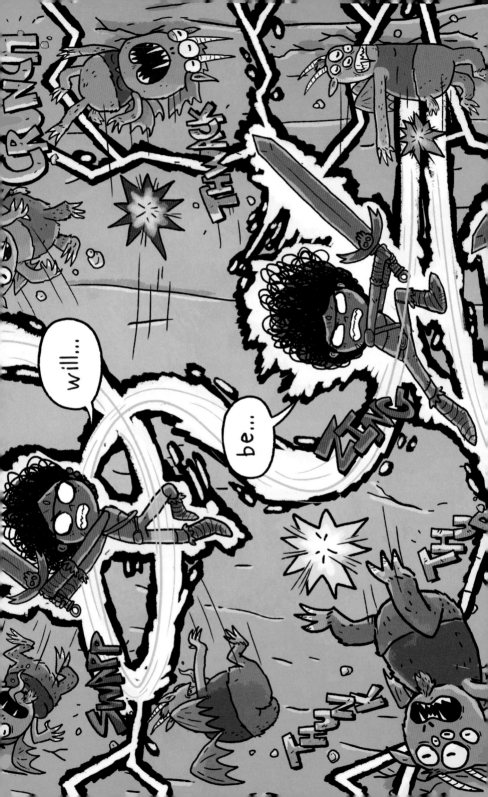

So tired.

RUMBLE RUMBLE RUMBLE

I gotcha, B!

:OOF!: Just woozy after my ZERK OUT!

RUMBLE RUMBLE RUMBLE

GAH!

KR-KR-KRACK!

KA-KOOM!

BARB!

PORK...

44

45

46

And last: **THE RAZOR BEAK RIDGE!**

Uhh....

Think the farmers would notice if we skipped this one?

P, what else you got in that sack?

Baby bird costumes!

PERFECT!

55

You can sit here.

It's not great but there's plenty of it.

GOBBLE

SLURP

MUNCH

FULL?

PAT PAT

BUUUU- yup-UURP! Finally.

Hey, who wants to hear the tale of how I lost my eye?

No.

Nah.

Booo.

I could tell the tale of how I met THIS fearsome beast.

Ooooo!

Cool!

Why not?

Yes!

Yeah!

Rad!

59

71

This sword is so RAD!

FWIP!

Uhhh... Suddenly feel weak.

Barb, that was AWESOME! Now use it AGAIN and bust us out of here!

cough

I...okay.

Here...goes. cough cough

BUURRRRRRRRRRRPPP!

HA HA HA HA HA HA HA HA HA HA HA HA HA HA HA HA HA HA

Ha ha, you two! I'll walk you to the northern pass!

HA! HA! My Shadow Bats have returned!

Do you have my...

She stopped you?!

And recovered the sword?!

Heh, heh, heh. Only a **FOOL** would send bats to catch a Berzerker.

A fool, eh?

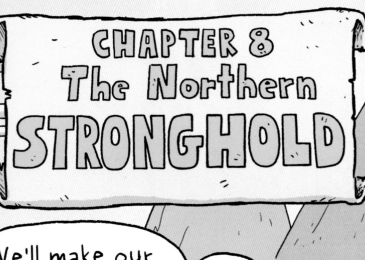

CHAPTER 8
The Northern
STRONGHOLD

We'll make our way north, along the Spire Path.

North it is!

I need some frost on my fur!

We gotta make up for lost time.

Hey, that reminds me of a song...

♪Frosty toes! ♪ I got frosty...

Barb... er...what's wrong?

Is it my singing?

PORKCHOP! You're OKAY!

Yeah.

Witch Head's creep?

Not so much.

BOOM!

AGAIN?

I see you're still palling around with monsters.

RRRRRRR.

Yes. He's my friend.

Don't worry, we'll fix your cart.

It says here...

COME SEE — ONE AND ALL

THE BIG **FIGHT!**

GROM THE GIANT! →

Vs.

← KATE (a farmer?)

KATE?!?

GRAB!

HEY!

P, we gotta go back!

Barb, your quest is over.

You tried. You don't have to stick your neck out anymore.

Don't you see, Porkchop, there isn't anyone else.

We are the only help there is.

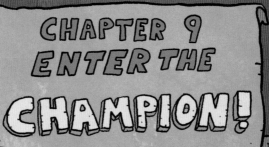

CHAPTER 9
ENTER THE
CHAMPION!

Kate, why did you challenge the SNOT GOBLINS to a FIGHT?

I'm sick of those dudes bullying us!

It's a total DRAG!

But now you gotta face their champion. He's a BEAST!

He will EAT you in one BITE!

He will STOMP you into JELLY!

He will TEAR you..

Thanks, Keith, I think I get it.

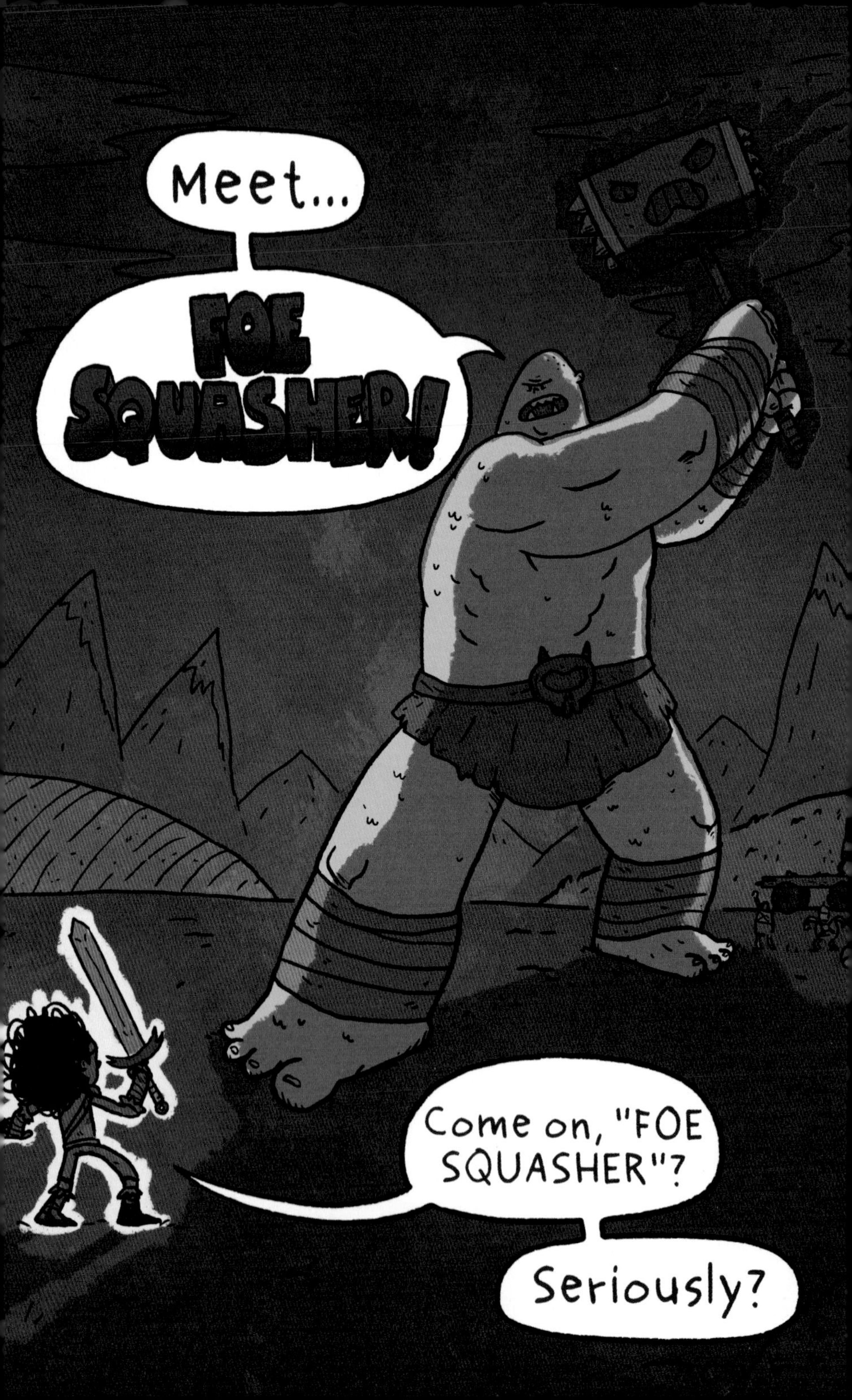
Meet...
FOE SQUASHER!
Come on, "FOE SQUASHER"?
Seriously?

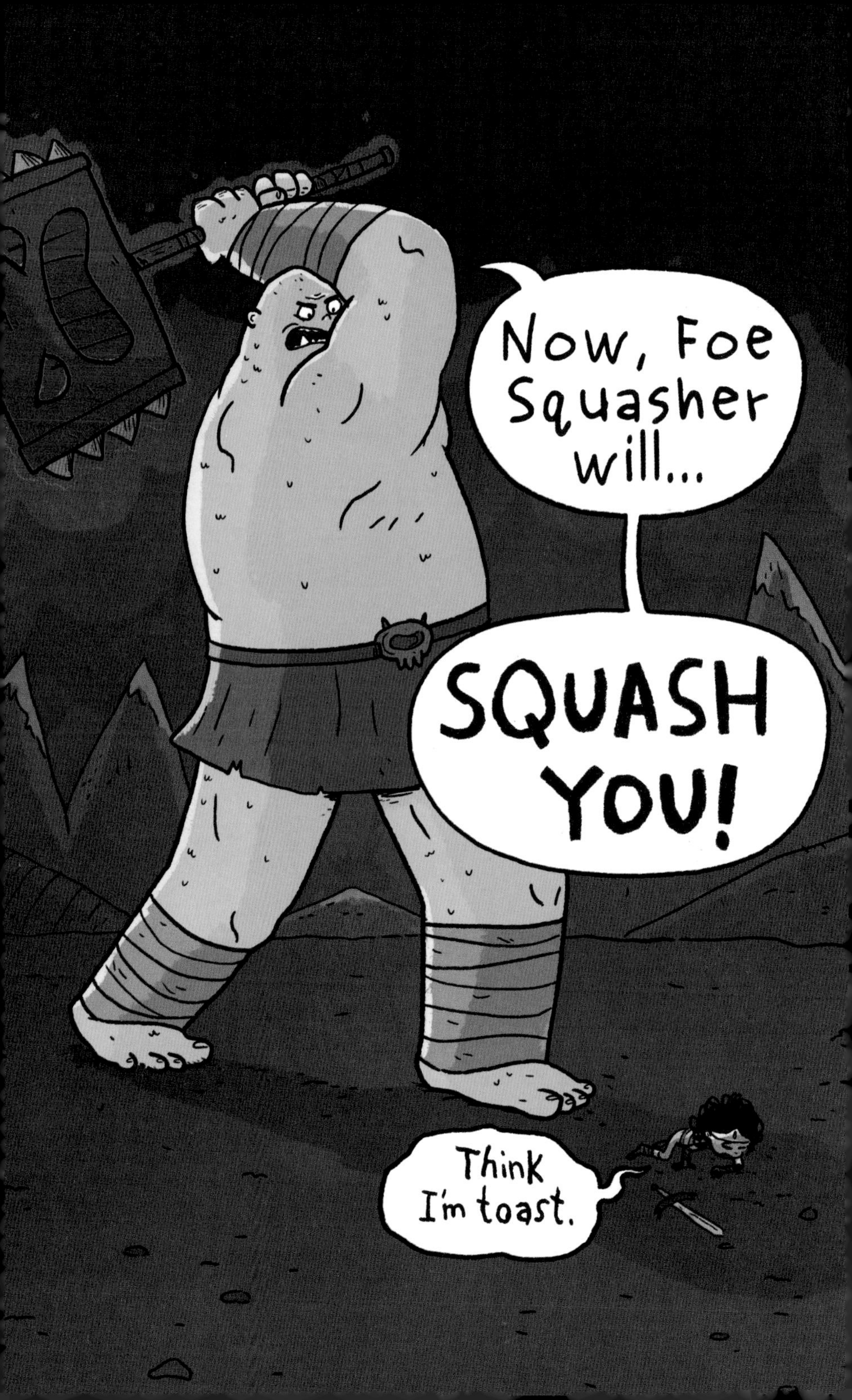
Now, Foe Squasher will...
SQUASH YOU!
Think I'm toast.

That joke was awful!
GROM HATES BAD JOKES!
AAAAAAAAA!
AAAA
You have to picture a giant bar of soap, then it's funny!
You know what, it doesn't matter. You're MAD!

I was the only Berzerker asked to join a SECRET meeting of the Wise Wizards. We pondered how to END the war with the monsters.
I am RAVEN, eader of the ZERKS. We can't win this war ALONE.
We are the Wise Wizards! Each member of this sacred council is a master of elemental MAGIC.
am GRAVEL STONE GRINDER! I say we hrow ROCKS at the monsters! Big ROCKS!
NO! FIREBALLS!
FRANNY FLAME FINGERS! That's your solution for EVERYTHING!
Just like a WATER mage to dismiss the power of FLAMES!
Mage?! I'm a WIZARD! You hotheaded FOOL!
I...I have an IDEA!

Witch Head tricked us and CAPTURED all the Zerks.

Barb, you're a Berzerker!

That's a great accomplishment.

But...I never wanted you to FIGHT in the Monster Wars.

Except me.

Funny thing about fighting monsters.

What?!

Since when are ZERKS and MONSTERS friends?

I actually made FRIENDS with one.

He...his name's PORKCHOP. He saved me from a GRUB. Big one. Then he gave me a lift...

WAIT!

The monster... SAVED you?!

Mum!
They alone know how to BEAT Witch Head.
Don't go!
You can SAVE us. All of us.
Please.
Look for the Wise Wizard FRANNY FLAME FINGERS.
She's hiding in the monster city of...

I have to save Bailiwick from Witch Head.

The key to stopping him is in Maug Horn.

It's going to be rough. So...

...I'm going alone.

Dan and Jason are a two-headed troll that grew up in Vermont. As a little two-headed troll they enjoyed smashing toys together, drawing comics, and joking around about stories and stuff. They were best pals back then and they are best pals today. Now fully grown, they still enjoy drawing comics and joking around, although they don't smash their toys together...as much. Check out their early reader graphic novel series Blue, Barry & Pancakes at all fine booksellers.